Empathy

Taylor Sapp

Alphabet Publishing

Contents

Before You Read

1. What is *empathy?* How is it different from *sympathy?*

2. Do you think you are a sympathetic or empathetic person?

3. Why is empathy important? Are there situations where having empathy is a problem?

4. Can empathy be learned?

5. Do you think empathy or kindness is linked to gender? If so, why and how?

Empathy

"What the heck is this?"

Rod had just walked in the door, coming home from work. He was staring at a small paper that greeted him on the dinner table right next to the door. It was a small piece of shiny black paper with white letters. Usually he was greeted by the smell of his wife's mediocre cooking, but today Judy was sitting on the couch watching TV.

"It's a coupon, honey."

If it was her doing, it was in his best interest to trash it quickly. However, curiosity got the best of Rod.

Holiday Special

PM

FREE CONSULTATION

We can modify
your personality to remove, add, or change any
parts of your
character to make a better you!

• Depression • Aggression

• Addiction • Anger Problems

• Disorders

BE THE <u>YOU</u> THAT YOU WANT TO BE!

When he'd first glanced at it, he'd been hoping for the best, $200 off at a hunting store, for instance. A gift certificate was certainly better than anything his wife could foul up getting.

Or so Rod thought.

"What the hell is PM?" he said, proud to not be keeping up on foolish expressions.

"That's Personality Modification, dear." Judy smiled at him innocently. She sounded a bit cunning, too. "You see, they had these two gentlemen on the Jenny Flowers Show today and..."

"And just what exactly does that mean?" Rage built as he was forced to walk to the refrigerator himself and get his own beer! He was too thrown off-guard by the change in routine to be angry, yet. He grabbed for a Brass City Brew and drained it in one swallow. He drank another beer before he'd even planted himself in his favorite armchair.

He switched away from her dumb talk show and found the football game.

"I'm empty," he said and held out the bottle toward his wife, who nodded and moved (too) slowly to the refrigerator.

And then it came on the TV during the half-time break: a stupid doctor talking about PM or whatever it was. With a free consultation!

Emasculation. Making him less of a real man!

That's what it was.

He'd heard stories: Johnny Bruno, former MMA-fighter, big tough guy. Then he'd met the wrong girl, who wanted to "fix a few things." Stop Johnny from spending every night at the bar, keep him from getting into a fights. OK, but the last word about old Johnny was he was teaching gym class in preschool and helping his daughters with their Girl Scout cookie runs!

Was his own wife trying to do that to him? Judy really didn't seem to realize who was the boss!

"You shouldn't drink when you're angry," his wife said.

He laughed, "What really gets me angry is when I run dry."

As she got to the fridge, he shouted, "And where is dinner?"

Judy would have attempted some apology but the impact of an empty beer bottle on her forehead stunned her as she stumbled backwards and fell to the floor.

Rod couldn't help laughing. She was a good 20 feet away. He'd made an excellent throw, though a perfect one would have hit her on the nose, or her always-yapping mouth.

"Did the bottle break?" he asked using sarcasm.

He heard his wife stumble to her feet, but the action of the game on TV was demanding most of his attention.

"Why are you so mean to me?" she murmured, through a stream of tears. There was a bunch more crying under her breath, ending with her typical "Why do I put up with this?" nonsense. Rod wasn't listening.

Unfortunately, that nosy and noisy Amanda Thompson was doing one of her videos outside the front window. She was one of these social media influencer types who was always filming stuff and yapping about how much better she was than her neighbors. Rod wished he could get his Rottweiler, Cold Cuts, to scare her off when she sat outside complaining about her 'trashy' neighbor. Anyway, Amanda had seen the fight through the giant living room window, pulled out her phone, and started filming. Then she called the cops.

Judy knew better than to open her mouth and say anything about him. But Amanda had caught the exact moment his bottle had so perfectly struck his wife's head on her video. So to his unfortunate surprise, just as the second half of the game was getting started, there was a knock at the door. Then Judy was walking two men in blue uniforms over. The two cops asked him about an incident or something with his wife. He nodded, attention still on the game, and he did his best to ignore the black cop.

Though Judy told them the cut on her head was from falling down the stairs, the police weren't convinced. In fact, even as they put him in handcuffs and led him out, he could feel the anger in him beginning to rise. He spent the afternoon in jail wondering if his wife and Amanda had planned this. What was Judy up to? She better not be touching his stuff. To make things worse, he could hear the game on the guards' radios. His team lost big.

When he got to court, the judge said, "You have two choices," in a tone that suggested there was only one:

Personality Modification.

Or prison.

He wanted to say prison out of spite and fear of what happened to old Johnny Bruno. But he knew what could happen to him in prison.

• • • • • • • • •

In the waiting room, there was a full house of weirdos. In front of him, an annoying brat whose parents couldn't discipline him ran around in circles. On one side, a blonde wearing very little clothing and lots of tattoos read a fashion magazine. "Drug addict, probably," Rod thought. On the other side of him, an Asian man in a dark business suit clutched his chair in a death grip. His knuckles were white. His face was also pale and he stared straight ahead with wide eyes and gritted teeth.

"Yo, fortune cookie, you ok?" He waved at the Asian who looked like he had some major anxiety.

Why was he here? These were real weirdos, not him. Rod was a decent, red-blooded man. He knew he was a jerk sometimes, but that's the way men were! His wife always knew that a bruise now and then meant he cared. Yeah, that coupon might have been her way of wanting him to be a bit more sensitive or some such nonsense. But since when did a man let a woman boss him around? His father taught him that. Dad always had a beer in one hand, the other hand in a fist to discipline his wife. Or his kid, if they stepped out of line.

Nothing wrong with that! Nothing wrong with being a man!

Rod stood up. "Forget this. She can accept it or not, but this is who I am." He pulled the court order out of his pocket. All he knew was what would happen if he didn't go through with this nonsense—48 hours in jail which would be just a warm-up to a 5- to 7-year prison term. He had watched enough TV to know bad things happened in prison. There were guys in there tougher than him that would eat him alive.

As he stood, crumpling the paper into a ball, on the edge of a key decision in his life, he was interrupted by a soft, fatherly voice.

"Mr. Rodney O'Leary? Anxious to get started, I see?"

He glared at the speaker, a bald, middle-aged man with a neat beard, dressed in an ugly Christmas sweater under his doctor's coat.

"I'm Dr. Norman Mann." He extended a hand which Rod did not bother to shake. Dr. Mann's smile didn't fade as he turned and waved to Rod to follow.

As Dr. Mann motioned him toward the door heading toward one fate, Rod took a final glance toward the exit, his last chance. Although he wasn't sure exactly what was going to happen, he had a strong feeling that it might be worse than prison. But instead of running, he just shook his head and followed the doctor inside.

Lying on a doctor's exam table in a small white room, Rod felt comfortable enough. He was bothered only by four small round metal circles checking his vitals, and a quieter, but still present, feeling of dread.

"I'm going to ask you some questions that will give us a baseline of where you are emotionally to make the necessary modifications."

"You mean emasculation, dontcha, Doc?" He spat on the ground for emphasis.

"If that's what you want to call it. You think that using that kind of language shows strength, but you are really using it to hide your weakness. You won't believe me now, but, Rod, I am going to make you stronger."

Rod snorted angrily and told the sad story of Johnny Bruno.

"You're talking about a brute who became a loving family man and father. What is so tragic about that?"

Everything, Rod wanted to say but he could see that he and the doc weren't going to agree.

"Don't even try to make me happy about this. Just shut up and get on with it, Doc."

Dr. Mann nodded and grabbed a few pictures off the nearby table. He held up a picture of a young boy whose face was all messed up. He had a giant nose and the eyes were uneven. The left eye was big and up near his forehead. The right eye was lower and was barely open. The top lip was bent up toward the nose in the middle. And his chin was basically not there.

Rod laughed nervously, out of instinct. He knew it was wrong to laugh, but the picture was simply too ridiculous for any other reaction. He expected the doctor to look angry, but instead Dr. Mann's smile seemed to grow even wider.

"You are probably aware that laughing at a picture of a boy with birth defects is wrong, but you have actually responded exactly as I would like. The reaction to this picture is either amusement or sympathy. When the modifications have been finished, it will be a useful litmus test of your progress."

"What are you saying, Doc? Do you want me to have a soft spot for ugly kids?"

"Oh no," Dr. Mann said, his smile getting wider, "You will be far, far beyond that."

The doctor continued with a series of questions, checking on a small screen in front of him and taking notes.

"How would you feel about cooking your wife a nice romantic dinner?"

"What if your wife asked you to stay home with the kids while she had a girl's night out?"

"What would you say if your wife asked you to join her in a candle-making class?"

For each question Rod laughed, replied with a short "Hell no!" or shook his head in disgust.

"Have you ever given to a homeless person on the street?"

"Hell no!"

"How about fed a homeless cat?"

"You mean kick them in the head!" He shivered, he hated cats, annoying pests not much better than rats,.

Dr. Mann nodded again, as if the answer was expected.

"What do cats have to do with anything?"

"Attitudes toward animals are an important component of empathy," the doctor replied without pause, like a true know-it-all jerk.

"Now just hold on. I'm not supposed to hit my wife or whatever, even though she knows when she deserves it. But it's the law. So you can make me stop hitting her, that's fine. But cats? What does that have to do with anything? Whatever answers I'm giving, I'm a man!"

The doctor's smile was calm and warm, but slightly amused. "You are going to realize how embarrassing you sound, Mr. O'Leary."

After the interview, Rod was taken to another room not much bigger than a closet. A comfortable-looking chair with a foot rest and pillow took up nearly the entire space. Attached to it was a single computer monitor as well as a few bags of colorful liquids. Were these some kind of powerful chemicals that would change his brain?

Rod wasn't sure what to say. The doctor sat him down and put a small metal ring over his head. He tapped on the computer screen as he sat on a stool (the only other piece of furniture in the room) and then smiled.

"You're in luck, Rod. You are an ideal candidate and this should be a really easy one."

He wasn't sure if he liked the sound of that.

"How soon will it be over? I was supposed to go duck hunting this afternoon."

The doctor laughed lightly. "This will only take minutes, not hours. Now I am going to have to put you to sleep. Much like with a computer, we're going to do a little reboot, restart your brain with a few little changes. I promise you will wake up feeling great. We're even going to clean up a few little problems in your brain so your general mood and memory should improve as well. Ok? Shall we proceed?"

The doctor reached for a needle with a tube attached to the liquids. He prepared Rod's right arm for the needle. But before he did, Rod angrily grabbed the doctor's hand.

"Doc, if you make me like cats, I will kill you."

To his surprise, the doctor nodded at him with the knowing smile of someone who'd seen the same reaction too many times before.

"I promise Rod, you are going to be thinking quite differently very soon."

· · · · ●· ● · · ·

It seemed too easy.

As he signed-out at the front desk, he didn't feel any different. In fact, he felt pretty good!

"I'm still me," he said quietly, confidently to himself. He couldn't tell what they'd done to him, but so far it was a lot better than going to prison! What had he been so worried about?

As he signed the papers to sign out, the receptionist was looking down, so she couldn't meet his smile. He desperately wanted her to share his good mood and hopefully add a spot of joy to her day. He saw a little button on her collar that said Rockin' Robin with a little bird playing a guitar, and he couldn't help but laugh.

"How cute!" he said. She must not have heard because she kept looking down, and he could find no name card. Addressing her without a name would be rude. His burst of energy started to lessen as he felt upset about not being able to give a compliment to the receptionist.

And then it went from bad to worse. He tried to concentrate on the form, hoping it would provide a short distraction. But the emotions remained, and the added pressure erupted on the pen, where he suddenly broke the tip on the sign-out form.

"Oh my God!" he exclaimed. At that the receptionist looked up. He held up the pen, now without a tip, and looked down in disgrace.

"Oh Miss, I am so sorry!" he began, "I feel it would be more polite if I could address you with a proper name."

At that, she smiled knowingly. Now they were sharing a moment. "It is Mrs. Adams, but Amy is fine."

Then he realized his prior exclamation of "Oh my God" might have been offensive, so he apologized for that as well. That out of the way, he returned to the bigger issue, ruining one of this poor lady's pens.

"Mrs. Adams! I am such a klutz. It appears I've broken your pen. You must tell me how to make amends."

His mind was swimming as he waited for her to answer. Money would be out of the question. Too crass. A replacement pen, or a whole box of them, would be an excellent idea, but he would have to leave to purchase them. What if she thought he was running off, debt unpaid?"

"That's okay, really. Consider the pen a gift for finishing your modification."

Although her expression was bright and honest and there was kindness in her voice, this did not make Rod feel better. In fact, her kindness only made his desire to make up for his mistake stronger.

He knew what a thankless job she must have, putting her health at risk by spending most of the day sitting down. And then there were all the questionable characters that she must deal with. What if they all broke or took her pens? Then what would be left? How much stress would that add to her day? Would she have to make a request to her boss for a replacement? What if she had to pay for the pens out of her own pocket? As a Mrs., she likely had children. She should be buying pens for them, not careless brutes with emotional issues. As these thoughts came together, Rod nearly wept, and he certainly would have if an answer had not struck his brain like a bolt of lightning!

But of course!

He pulled out the expensive pen that had been a gift from his father. It had lasted him seven or so good years, was of a far higher quality than these cheap throw away pens, and most importantly, was near unbreakable.

"If you'll take this pen, Mrs. Adams, you shouldn't have such problems with any other brutes like myself. It was a gift from my father, and though I carry it around regularly, I rarely put it to use, and it would assist you much better in your profession."

Mrs. Adams shook her head. "A gift from your father? I can't take that." Her words were kind but her tone was a bit flat.

He smiled. "Please do not worry. The circumstances in which my father *gave* me this pen were not the happiest and I would prefer to forget them."

Rod had, in fact, stolen the pen. His white lie about how he had acquired the pen was wrong. The fact that he couldn't return the pen because his father was deceased was worse. Giving it to this poor woman might be the best way to ensure a good home for it and clear his conscience. Suddenly he was flooded with shame. He remembered his past pride at stealing the pen, his feeling of relief when his father passed, and his deep regret that he could not repair the relationship now!

Rod realized he was weeping. He blew his nose on a tissue, closed his eyes, and took several deep but uneven breaths. After calming down, he handed over the pen and began telling the receptionist about his father and the pen. But as he looked at Mrs. Adams' eyes, he could detect annoyance.

"Oh my! I am talking too much!" The last thing this poor lady needed was a man wasting her time! She certainly must be quite busy. "Is there anything you'd like to share that troubles you? I know I am a stranger, but in case you're not getting enough of an opportunity to ..." he asked.

"Thank you," She interrupted him by holding her hand up. "I know this is all new for you, Mr. O'Leary, but keep in mind, I meet patients like yourself twenty-times a day. And now that we're past lunch, I've had enough time to discuss my feelings and my early childhood." It sounded as if she'd made this same speech many times before.

"Apologies! I simply leave the pen and say good-day. Would that help you continue your afternoon in the best fashion?"

She nodded and smiled again. "I appreciate the gift. Your wife is going to be thrilled, Mr. O'Leary." She never got tired of saying that.

· · · · ● · ● · · ·

Judy knew things had changed when he apologized for making her wait, the first time he had ever apologized to her! The feeling became clearer on the drive home. They must have stopped at least five times to avoid hitting any squirrels or other animals in the road, which her husband had once called, depending on their condition, "vermin" or "dinner".

"Poor little guy!" He'd spotted a possum on the road, obviously injured from getting hit by a car. Rod insisted on stopping, picking him up gently in his jacket, and asking his wife to google the nearest animal hospital.

On the way, Rod watched the road and found a raccoon in terrible shape. When he got to the animal hospital, he was told by an annoyed vet that both were already dead, and that they only treated pets and not wild animals.

"You did your best, dear."

"It's horrible." Rod's eyes were red and tear-stained.

The next morning, Rod brought her breakfast in bed along with her slippers. He'd also made her a nice cup of green tea, something he'd previously hated. He associated green tea with the Japanese and hated it in honor of his grandfather's military service and prejudice. Not to mention, Rod saw tea in general as 'gay' as well as any form of coffee that wasn't strictly black.

But now? As he buttered her whole-wheat toast and rubbed her shoulders, it was like a dream, a wonderful dream. But Judy would eventually have to wake up.

• • • •• • •• • • • •

Dr. Mann listened to her concerns patiently with a smile that he never dropped, as if waiting to give his usual assurances to confused house-wives who strangely found themselves missing the old violent brutes who had barely qualified as "husbands".

"Let me put it this way," he said when she fin-ished, "if you have laser eye surgery done on your eyes, can they correct your eye to 20-20, or do they give you a choice, 20-30/20-40, for example? Think of it like this: your husband was balanced before but on the opposite side of the scale, as if he were nearsighted. He was a nearly perfect ideal of an insensitive person. So in order to make things work correctly, we had to make an extreme shift. Now you're going to have to get over your issues, not his. I don't want to get into your past, but victims of abuse often feel that they almost miss the abuse. Quite simply, you've been accustomed to abuse, not kindness. This is a textbook PM situation."

"So I'm going to have to learn to accept him fully?"

The doctor shook his head. "I'm afraid that rarely works. I've seen the same thing happen all too often. The good news is there is a solution, and it almost always works."

• • • ● • ● ● • • ••

When Judy came in, Rod rushed to her bleeding cheek immediately, his arms filled with various bandages, creams, ice packs, and other medical equipment.

"Oh honey, honey." His eyes were damp and filled with concern.

"It was that brute Kyle Johnson. He threw a can of beer. Luckily, he'd already drunk it first."

"I just talked to his wife the other day. He's got a court-ordered PM coming up soon."

"Thank goodness." Judy said.

Rod was so impressed by his brave wife! Every day, she was at another rally, another march against injustice, defending civil rights, protesting guns, or whatever. She fought the battles that he did not have the stomach for. Instead he spread his love in all the ways he could; in this case, a quiche should refresh her SJW (Social Justice Warrior) spirit. As he thanked all of the many gods and religions he now respected (how prejudiced to follow only one) he remembered with dismay that he hadn't thanked his doctor in almost two weeks. Luckily, a new batch of cookies in the oven would soon be on the way along with a lovely note.

As he burst out in tears, overwhelmed by these many emotions, his wife knowingly provided her shoulder. How thankful she was for this support, his love, and his empathy.

Glossary

baseline: a starting point to use to compare things to

batch: a group of things made at the same time

brat: a child with very bad manners

brute: a rude person who can be violent

coupon: a paper that gives you a discount for a product or service

damnit: an interjection that people use when they are frustrated or upset

emasculation: the process of making a man feel weak

empathy the ability to share the feelings of another

exclamation: words said suddenly to show emotion

influencer: a person who posts on social media that other people follow and admire

jerk: a foolish or mean person

klutz: a clumsy person

litmus test: (here) a way of testing whether something worked or not

masculinity: the qualities of being a man, often meaning being tough, strong, and unemotional

nearsighted: unable to see things faraway clearly

red-blooded: energetic, full of life

trashy: people who are seen as lower quality

vitals: signs of health such as heartbeat and temperature

yap: to talk in a loud annoying way

After You Read

1. Describe the 2 main characters, Rod and his wife.

2. What is their relationship like in the beginning of the story?

3. How does their relationship change after Rod gets Personality Modification?

4. How does it change again at the end?

5. Why do the police come for Rod?

6. What is Rod's punishment?

7. How does he feel about this punishment?

8. How does his conversation with the of-

fice manager show the changes to Rod's personality?

9. What other changes do we see in Rod's life?

10. What problem does his wife face? What is the resolution?

11. How is the relationship between Rod and his wife different at the end?

12. This story is written from the point of view of Rod. That means he describes the events and people from his perspective, which is filled with sexism, racism, and other extreme prejudices. How would a more objective narrator describe the fight with his wife and the people at the clinic?

13. Do you think PM will ever really exist? Do you think it's a good idea? What are the advantages and dangers of PM?

14. What are some more realistic ways to deal with people whose cruelty hurts other people?

Writing

Write what happens next. Are Rod and his wife finally happy? How do they live now? Do they need to get PM again for any reason?

More Readers

Baby Shopping
Changes
Empathy
English Class on Mars
Ghost in My Room
Magic Employment Agency
Rebirth
Attack of the Sleep Demon
The AI Therapist
Thought Police
Time Travel Research: Genghis Khan
Virtual Unreality

AlphabetPublish.com/Book-Category/
Graded-Reader